OTHER BOOKS BY THE SAME AUTHOR AND ARTIST

written by Alvin Tresselt and illustrated by Roger Duvoisin

HIDE AND SEEK FOG

SUN UP

written by Alvin Tresselt and illustrated by Yarolslava

THE MITTEN

written and illustrated by Roger Duvoisin

SPRING SNOW

written by Mary Calboun and illustrated by Roger Duvoisin

THE NINE LIVES OF HOMER C. CAT

WOBBLE THE WITCH' CAT

written by Priscilla and Otto Friedrich and illustrated by Roger Duvoisin

THE WISHING WELL IN THE WOODS

written by Charlotte Zolotow and illustrated by Roger Duvoisin

IN MY GARDEN

THE POODLE WHO BARKED IN THE WIND

WAKE UP, FARM!

by ALVIN TRESSELT

Pictures by ROGER DUVOISIN

A WORLD'S WORK CHILDREN'S BOOK

First published in Great Britain in 1966 by
The World's Work (1913) Ltd
The Press at Kingswood, Tadworth, Surrey

Printed by Litografía A. Romero, S. A.
Santa Cruz de Tenerife
Islas Canarias

To Ellen Victoria and India Rachel

All through the night, while the bright stars shine
in the sky, everything sleeps.
Birds in their nests and cows in the fields.
Horses in barns and children in their beds.
Now it is time for the sun to come up, and the sky grows bright
First one, then two, then all the birds
begin to sing their morning songs.
Wake up, Farm!

The big fat rooster
hears them and he hops up
on the fence post.
Cock-a-doodle-doo! he crows.
Wake up, Farm!

Cluck, cluck, cluck, the chickens wake up.

They hop down on the ground and start to eat corn.

The horse wakes up in her stall and licks

her baby colt behind the ears.

The white ducks waddle out of the bushes.

They wriggle their tails and jump into the brook for a swim.

Quack, quack, quack!

Wake up, Farm!

Grunt, grunt. The roly-poly pigs wake up and root about their pen looking for breakfast.

The grey goose sticks her long neck out of her nest

in the grass and looks around.

Honk, honk, honk!

Wake up, Farm!

Then high in the apple tree the turkey wakes up, too.

He ruffles his feathers and calls,

Gobble, gobble, gobble!

Wake up, Farm!

The donkey hears all the noise and opens his big brown eyes.

He looks very sleepy as he wriggles his long soft ears.

Now the sheep and baby lambs come out of the sheepfold to eat the wet shiny grass.

The strutting pigeons fly out of the dovecote
and circle over the big red barn.

Coooo, coooo, coooo!

Wake up, Farm!

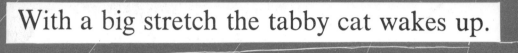

With a big stretch the tabby cat wakes up.

She purrs as she gives her kittens their morning bath.

Here is the dog, wide awake and barking at a squirrel.

Bow, wow, wow!

Wake up, Farm!

A warm furry rabbit wakes up in the rabbit hutch.

He twitches his wriggly nose as he eats a carrot for breakfas

Buzz, buzz, buzz!
The buzzy bees come out of their hives
and buzz around the pink clover.

The cows are awake and waiting by the pasture gate.

Moo, moo, moo! It's time for milking!

And here comes the farmer with his shiny milk pails just as the sun comes over the hill.

At last a little boy in the big farmhouse wakes up and stretches.

The birds are singing and the animals are calling.

The bright morning sun is shining in the window.

And mother calls from the kitchen, "Breakfast!"

Another day has begun. Good morning!